I NEVER TOLD
And Other Poems

I NEVER TOLD

And Other Poems

Myra Cohn Livingston

MARGARET K. McELDERRY BOOKS
New York

Maxwell Macmillan Canada
Toronto

Maxwell Macmillan International
New York   Oxford   Singapore   Sydney

For Alice, Ann, April, Deborah,
John, Karen, Kris, Martha, Monica,
Pat, Peg, and Tony

Margaret K. McElderry Books
Macmillan Publishing Company
866 Third Avenue
New York, NY 10022

Maxwell Macmillan Canada, Inc.
1200 Eglinton Avenue East
Suite 200
Don Mills, Ontario M3C 3N1

Macmillan Publishing Company is part of the
Maxwell Communication Group of Companies.
First edition
Printed in the United States of America
10 9 8 7 6 5 4 3 2 1

Library of Congress Cataloging-in-Publication Data
Livingston, Myra Cohn.
I never told and other poems / Myra Cohn Livingston. — 1st ed.
p.   cm.   Summary: A collection of
poems offering imaginative observations of everyday things.
ISBN 0-689-50544-2
1. Children's poetry, American. [1. American poetry.]   I. Title
PS3562.I945I18   1992   811'.54—dc20   91-20475

CONTENTS

BEGGAR

This wind
will follow you
around a cold corner,
chase you down the street until you
leave it

waiting
at your front door,
blowing its breath through cracks,
howling through chinks, begging to come
inside.

Black River

Black snake
swallowed water
swallowed dark

bloated
himself heavy
with water

sinking
under the bridge
slowly he

became
black water
black river

CALGARY

Printing ideograms

in a
wild sky

Canada geese
spill out in

V's

CANDLE

Inside the yellow
flame, a blue shadow struggles to
wriggle itself free

sending little puffs
of black smoke into the air;
waving side to side,

jumping up, changing
from fat to thin, dropping small
tears of melted wax,

sighing, sighing, blown
out by the wind, vanishing
into a black wick.

CIRCUS CLOWN

In striped pajamas,
round red nose,
a pointed cap,
patched cheeks, bare toes.

In floppy gloves,
big ears of red,
green curls around
a bald white head.

In baggy pants
and painted frown,
it must be hard
to be a clown.

CLOSET

Under the stairs, a secret cave
heaped with treasure waits for me,
waits for my *Open Sesame!*

I turn the knob. The brown door creaks.
I shine my flashlight. Looming shapes—
forty thieves wrapped in dusty capes—
hail my return. I crouch and count
ingots of silver, bars of gold,
all that my robber fingers hold.

Brocades and silks from strange bazaars,
translucent pearls and diamonds bright
glitter within my beam of light.
I reach for the doorknob, making sure
I can escape if anyone dares
tread on my cave roof, under the stairs.

CRICKETS

they	tell
the	time
of	night
they	tick
the	time
of	night
they	tick
they	tell
of	night
they	tick
and	tell
the	time
they	tick
they	tell
the	time
they	click

First Flight

I wondered how it looked,
   that sea to shining sea,
   that purple mountain's majesty,

   those amber waves and fruited plain,
   those spacious skies of blue,

   and then, I flew.

Flying West

Someone raked the gray, brushed earth of Utah,
poured phosphorus over the red walls of Bryce Canyon,
caught an eagle in Zion, made it into a blue lake.

Someone shaped the Colorado River like a genie's lamp,
painted the Devil's Playground white,
sewed ruffles around Lake Mead

but never saw this from the air.

GIVE ME BOOKS, GIVE ME WINGS

Give me books,
give me wings,
let me fly
from the page
to a once-upon time
in a long-ago age;
taking off
for an extraterrestrial
place
with brave words
for my flight
through the darkness
of space;
gliding
down
to an ocean's
mysterious
deep
with watery shadows
and pictures to keep;
soaring back
to the earth
and a world
that I know;
give me books,
give me wings
to climb higher
and grow.

I NEVER TOLD

Nobody knew where Gregory hid.
I looked for him. I really did.

Out near the stream where we always wade,
the place where the bushes make dark shade,
over the fence and up in our tree,
behind the elms, but I couldn't see
where he had gone. Then I heard him say

Leave me alone. Don't give me away.

He said it again with a sort of sigh.
He said it again with a little cry.

So I ran on back where the others stood.
I shrugged my shoulders.

I've looked. No good.

I didn't glance back to where he hid.
And I never told. I never did.

I Would Have Come

You could have called,
Picked up the phone.
I wasn't busy.
I was alone.

Nothing to do.
Just sitting there
Right by the phone,
Right in my chair.

You could have called.
I was at home.
If you had called
I would have come.

JUST ONCE

Right off the
road, a narrow path
winds down to where an iron gate
stands open. There, far down below
is where I go.

A deer came
near the rusty gate
just once. I didn't get too close
but watched her nibbling on the ground
without a sound.

Another time
I saw raccoons
but I keep hoping one day soon
the deer will come back to the gate
and so I wait.

Kansas Visit

This land is nothing that I know,
A herd of circling buffalo
Penned in a ring of summer sun;

Red barns, white farms,
A grove of elms,
Miles and miles of space to run;

Haystacks yellow in the fields,
The lonesome whistle of a train
And clacking wheels.

LASIOCAMPIDAE

In the
wide crotches of
branches, on the tenderest
twigs, tent caterpillars lay their
larvae,

building
webs of camp tents
stretched between trees, covered
with endless yards of mosquito
netting.

MACAW

Even
the quiet blue
feathers of the parrot
cannot silence his brash yellow
squawking

MARCH NIGHT

Raindrops,
clinging to the
holes of my window screen,
pretend for a moment they are
diamonds.

Moon: Two Views

1.

Sliced in half, the moon
tips on her right side, bleeding
trails of white chalk dust.

2.

Looking into a
dark midnight river, moon sees
no one but herself.

MORNING AT MALIBU

Here, in Malibu Beach,
it is morning,
        morning,
gray morning,
silver morning,
morning of fog and mist,

and only the birds know morning is alive!

NIAGARA: CANADIAN HORSESHOE FALLS
(For Marian Reiner)

in   spray
  my   wet
    ears   a
      a   face
    roaring   my
       in   in
        my   mist
         eyes   fine
          a

```
f       c       s       p
a       a       o       o
l       l       u       u
l       l       n       n
i       i       d       d
n       n       i       i
g       g       n       n
                g       g
```

water   water   water   water   water   water   water   water

and everything is white

Night Flight over Kansas

It is
the moon, polished
white on the cold wing of
a jetliner, staring down at
herself

through the
dark night of a
Kansas winter, finding
her reflection dipping as she
dances.

NIGHT OF THUNDER

She dreams a night of thunder
Rumbling until day.
Covering her misted face
She slowly fades away,

Wrapping herself in silver,
Disappearing soon
Into a tangled web of clouds
She falls asleep. The moon.

Notes on a Bee

Stuck on
the window screen,
his five eyes fix on me.
His feet, hooked into the wire mesh
hang on

for dear
life, thin wings still,
stripes of yellow and black
on his stomach undulating.
He makes

a slow
turn, unhooks two
feet, turns sideways, and is
gone, flying off without even
a buzz.

OLD SPIDER WEB

Dust settles on the spider's web,
on littered insects, trapped within.
Dust on silk threads stretched taut and thin.

Dust covers the spider's spinnerets
under the dusty window sill.
Dust on the spider, dust on her kill.

OUR CHRISTMAS TREE

I picked it out,
Our Christmas tree,
The tallest one that I could see.

We brought it home,
Strung on the lights
And decorated it last night.

I like to lie
Upon the floor
And think where it had been before

In forests,
Spreading branches wide
Dreaming of ornaments to hide.

QUEENSBORO BRIDGE

Lights are
gardens bursting
over the blue-ridged hills
of the

rolling
Queensboro Bridge;
yellow chrysanthemums
and white

roses
plucked from the
endless fields, twinkling with
scarlet

like a
bed of colored
flowers blooming the whole
night long

Rocky Mountains: Colorado

Meringues
with pointed tops,
iced with confectioner's sugar,
stand tall, pinching themselves into
gorges.

S: Silent Shark

The silent
  shark
the scaly
  shark
  is
  searching
  out
  a
  seal

  he'll swim
  and stalk
  and snap
  and snare

  and scrunch
  his sumptuous
  meal.

September Garden

Good-bye to the summer.
The zinnias are gone.
Patches of brown lie dead on the lawn.

Tomato vines wither.
Daisies turn brown.
Pansies are dying. The dahlias droop down.

Impatiens are wilting.
No lilies in sight,
But chrysanthemums uncurl in purple and white.

Shortcut

I know a shortcut
through the bushes,
out beyond the hollow rushes,
where the water lies so blue,
where some flies lay eggs in water,
where they cling there under cover.
Dragonflies wait there and hover.

We can watch them.
Just we two.

6:15 A.M.

Two crows
    wake me
      flying
      crying

over the hills;

two black crows
    scratching
    snatching

at the earth;

two carrion crows
    scolding
    folding

their black wings;

two black carrion crows
    perching
    searching

through the dirt
    for something
    anything

to eat.

SOMETHING STRANGE

When no one else
   can understand
I get Charlie.
We just stand
looking,
listening to the sound
of something moving all around.
Charlie has to sniff the ground.

When no one else
   can feel it near,
it's Charlie
who will always hear.
Bristles rise up through his hair.
He points his tail up in the air.

We both know something strange is there.

Song of Peace

Sing aloud
If sing you can,

Sing of woman,
Sing of man.

Sing of peace,
Sing of child.

Sing aloud.
Sing wild.

Statue of Liberty

Give me your tired, your poor, she says,
Those yearning to be free.
Take a light from my burning torch,
The light of Liberty.

Give me your huddled masses
Lost on another shore,
Tempest-tossed and weary,
These I will take and more.

Give me your thirsty, your hungry
Who come from another place.
You who would dream of freedom
Look into my face.

STATUES

The
statues
stand
so tall,
so still,
so quiet   in the grass,

that
I am
tall
and I am
still
and quiet.   Then, I pass.

Summer Daisies

July
daisies are bright
yellow faces looking
at the sun, their white hair combed long
and straight.

August
daisies turn brown
and wither, their tangled hair
mussing up, bleaching gray in the
sunlight.

10 P.M.

This is the time of gentle rain.
Darkness all around.
A drop upon the windowpane.
A drop upon the ground.

The moment after lightning,
A time to hold, to keep
Against the coming frightening
Black thunderstorms of sleep.

THE BIGGEST QUESTIONS

Guns
and
rifles

who will buy them?

Jets
and
fighters

who will fly them?

Tanks
and
helmets

who will make them?

War
and
battles

who forsake them?

THE DIFFERENCE

Grandfather's chair
    is where he sits.
Grandfather's chair
    is where he fits.

    Nobody else would ever dare
    Think of sitting in Grandfather's chair.

Grandmother's chair
    is where she sits.
Grandmother's chair
    is where she knits.

    Somebody else could try her chair.
    Grandmother says she doesn't care.

The Dream

My arms
turn into wings.
I raise them up slowly,
waving them toward the tall ceiling,
pushing

my toes
against the floor,
flapping my wings faster
until I feel myself soaring,
flying.

THE GAME

Plastic soldiers march on the floor
Off to fight a terrible war.

The green troops charge. The gray side falls.
Guns splatter bullets on the walls.

Tanks move in. Jet fighters zoom
Dropping bombs all over the room.

All the soldiers are dead but two.
The game is over. The war is through.

The plastic soldiers are put away.
What other game is there to play?

THIS BOOK IS MINE

This book is mine.
I checked it out.
I read it
and found all about
another me
who lived before,
who opened up a magic door,
who sailed an ocean,
flew a plane,
a me
I never could explain
until I found myself
within
a story
where
I've always
been.